Graham Handley and Stanley King

Brodie's Notes on Graham Greene's

The Quiet American

Pan Books London and Sydney

First published 1980 by Pan Books Ltd
Cavaye Place, London SW10 9PG
1 2 3 4 5 6 7 8 9
© Graham Handley and Stanley King 1980
ISBN 0 330 50177 1
Filmset in Great Britain by
Northumberland Press Ltd, Gateshead, Tyne and Wear
Printed and bound by
Richard Clay (The Chaucer Press) Ltd, Bungay, Suffolk

Contents

Page references in these Notes are to the Penguin edition of
The Quiet American, but as Parts and Chapters are also identified,
the Notes may be used with any edition of the book

To the Student

A close reading of the set book is the student's primary task. These Notes will help to increase your understanding and appreciation of the novel, and to stimulate *your own* thinking about it: *they are in no way intended as a substitute* for a thorough knowledge of the book.

The author and his work

Graham Greene, one of the most distinguished and prolific of contemporary writers, was born in 1904. He was educated first at Berkhamsted School, where his father was Headmaster, and later at Balliol College, Oxford, where he was awarded an exhibition in Modern History. In 1925 he came down from Oxford, having published a book of verse while still there. From Oxford he went to Nottingham, where he served his apprenticeship in journalism. In 1926 Greene was converted to Roman Catholicism. For three years he worked as a sub-editor on *The Times*, and in 1929 his first novel, *The Man Within* appeared.

Novels, stories and 'entertainments' (his own term for the writing he regarded as different in serious intention from his more considered work) appeared at regular intervals. *Stamboul Train* (1932) established his early reputation, which was confirmed and reinforced in 1935 with the publication of *England Made Me*. There is little point in providing a catalogue of Greene's publications, but it is perhaps appropriate to indicate his range and his main concerns. All except one of his novels and a number of short stories have been filmed, and in 1975 some of these stories were adapted for television in the series *Shades of Greene*. In 1966 he was made a Companion of Honour.

As early as 1935 there emerged one clear indication of his future pattern of work: having travelled in Liberia he published an account of his experiences in *Journey Without Maps*. From then on Greene's area of interest might be described as global. No contemporary writer of note has travelled so variously, so widely, nor has any writer succeeded in capturing both local and racial atmosphere more truthfully. One of his most harrowing novels, *The Power and the Glory* (1940) is set in Mexico; the action of *The Heart of the Matter* (1948) takes place in West Africa, while the book you are about to study, *The Quiet American* (1955) is set in Vietnam and has Saigon as its political and moral centre. Here the student's attention is drawn particularly to the section on 'Background' which follows immediately upon this introduction: no one can read *The Quiet American* without some knowledge of the particular significance of its local setting, despite the universality of its themes and situations. In *A Burnt-Out Case* (1961) Greene goes back to Africa, while *Our Man in Havana* spells out its own location; and in the earlier film script of *The Third Man* Greene uses the architectural backcloth of post-war Vienna for the setting of his human drama.

Greene's geographical identification is remarkable. Whether the background – and foreground – is Brighton, a provincial Argentinian town, or Saigon, his touch is sure, his observation discriminating, both visually and psychologically. He has the journalist's eye and facility of expression.

It must be said, however, that the great novelist should possess talents correspondingly greater than these; he must be interested in people as individuals, forever fascinated by the multiplicity of human nature in all its degraded and elevated forms, and he has to be concerned for the spirit and soul as well as for the body.

It is impossible to read Graham Greene's novels without becoming aware of his strong Roman Catholic convictions. He has contrasted the Protestant attachment to *good works* with the Roman Catholic emphasis on *faith* and preoccupation with *mortal sin*, and often in his novels he examines the problem of sin in the human condition. But behind Greene the Roman Catholic is Greene the humanitarian, aware of frailty and temptation, and of the sordid, deprived lives where religion has neither power, glory nor even effect – apart from the only dimly-comprehended manifestations of ritual. In many of the books the dogmas of Catholicism are present, bulking large for instance in the consciousness of Scobie in *The Heart of the Matter*, and in the fears and admissions of the whisky priest in *The Power and the Glory*. They are also present in the soured and bitter virginity of Pinkie in *Brighton Rock*. They are not, however, at the centre of *The Quiet American*, where the codes of involvement and reportage, of feeling and rationality, battle for the human soul like the terrible conflicts witnessed by the fictional protagonists. Greene has no propagandist intention, no assertion of right and wrong; he presents a faithful record of human nature in action, but never without sympathy.

For whether or not his characters are involved in spiritual or obsessional decision, Greene always manages to identify with his fictional creatures through the quality of his own compassion for suffering humanity. It is a sympathy for the state of man: though a character may finish with the technical full-stop, a question-mark is left in the reader's mind beyond the pages of the book. How are they to be judged, those who sinned and killed and followed the dictates of self or a false ideology? Their particular situation may be foreign to us but their reactions occupy that common area of experience, real or vicarious, which colours the world of life and the living world of the imagination.

Graham Greene's mode of expression is journalistic in the best sense, but perhaps we should look more closely at the high degree of technical and imaginative art involved. The reasons for the filming of so much of his writing are obvious. He has a fine sense of the dramatic, seen in the narrative tension of his novels and stories. There is always something *happening*: violence, the un-expected, the grotesque, the funny, the horrible and horrifying, the last two being markedly present in *The Quiet American*. Emotions are on or near the surface, yet platitude and cliché are skilfully avoided.

Greene is adept at psychological exposure, and though his characters may be far from home they reflect the early con-ditioning of that home, and retrospect plays a large part in their lives. Relationships are investigated in scrupulous and telling detail, whether deeply or in passing, and the habit which irritates or endears is given a selective focus.

It has been said of Greene that he is too concerned with the sordid or degrading rather than with the elevating; there is some truth in this, as you will see from your reading of *The Quiet American*. Yet much of life is exactly as he sees it – his approach is neither sensational nor sentimental, but shows a clear awareness of motive and behaviour. Sexuality and spirituality are the pivots of a Greene novel, though *The Quiet American* has the much broader basis of humanity for its balance. There may be little beauty in the appraisal, but there is truth; you may be repelled by an incident or an emphasis, but you will never be bored.

The Quiet American has an interesting structure and some difficult-ies of plot, and these will be examined in the sections which follow; the book is marked by its use of retrospect, the kind of technique employed effectively by film-makers over the last fifty years. But if the technical achievements of *The Quiet American* are impressive, the sense of place, the stronger sense of identity with man in his self-revelation and above all, the underlying concern at what should concern us all, these are the major facets of a fine, exciting and moving novel. It is somewhat ironic that one of Greene's latest novels should be called *The Human Factor*; it is a title and an emphasis that admirably fits the author's exploration and definition in *The Quiet American*.

Further reading

Other novels by Graham Greene, particularly:

Brighton Rock (Penguin)

The Heart of the Matter (Penguin)

The Human Factor (Penguin)

Our Man in Havana (Penguin)

The Stamboul Train (Penguin)

Background

Modern maps may not show the provinces of French Indo-China bordering on the South China Sea (though they should still show Laos and Cambodia), so the following rough definition of their limits may be of help. *Tonkin* is mountainous and heavily forested. Bounded to the north by China, to the west by Laos and to the east by the Gulf of Tonkin: the southernmost area is around Phat Diem. The main town is Hanoi, the principal waterways the Black and the Red Rivers and the main highway, route coloniale 4. *Annam* is rich in rice and other produce, but also forested and with a range of mountains parallel to the coast of the South China Sea. The province extends from the southern border of Tonkin to Phan Tiet, which is east of, and roughly level with, Saigon. It is bounded on the west by Laos, Cambodia (now sometimes called Kampuchea) and Cochin China, and to the east, the South China Sea. One of the coastal towns was Hue, where Phuong's father had been a mandarin. *Cochin China* is also rich in rice, and contains a fair amount of swamp-land. Bounded to the north by Cambodia, to the east partly by Annam and partly by the South China Sea and to the west by the Gulf of Thailand. Saigon is its main town.

The Annamese, of mixed Mongolian and Indonesian blood, threw off Chinese rule in the tenth century AD after more than a thousand years of strongly resisted domination. They extended their empire to take in a large part of what became French territory and were ruled by a strongly nationalistic dynasty (the last representative of which was the Emperor Bao Dai on whom Fowler was such an authority).

French and Portuguese traders and missionaries began to take an interest in the area in the sixteenth century, and the French were sufficiently well established by the nineteenth century to be ceded three eastern provinces of Cochin China in 1862; after 1874 Cochin China was administered as a French colony. The French eventually (1887) occupied Annam, Tonkin, Cambodia and Laos and placed these, with Cochin China, under the control of a governor-general. Although the new provinces prospered, there was always a strong nationalist movement, which was eventually to owe much to the son of an official in Annam. Born in 1892 as Nguyen Sinh Cung and known for many years as Nguyen Ai Quoc he later became Ho Chi Minh.

After training in different parts of the world Ho Chi Minh returned to Tonkin during the 1939–45 war and, with the aid of Chinese Nationalists, formed a resistance group, part of which was the Vietminh, armed (unofficially) by the American OSS (Office of Strategic Services). Their job was to help fugitive American airmen and to harry the Japanese army which had by now gained control of Cochin China and Annam for the purpose of attacking Burma. The local French general had appealed to the USA for arms to resist the Japanese. This aid was refused and the Vichy government in France decided that the Japanese entry should not be opposed.

In 1945 President de Gaulle ordered the repossession of French Indo-China. The Japanese disarmed the French troops and interned them. French civilians were humiliated and killed. When the Japanese left, the local Vietminh came out into the open and savagely killed many French (and pro-French natives) until British forces intervened.

From then on the position became intensely complicated – too much so, in fact, to be dealt with in any detail here. When Pyle first comes on the scene, Ho Chi Minh has just occupied Hanoi, been thrown out, and is attacking the French in Tonkin in divisional (10000 men) strength in several places; in Annam and Cochin China, guerrilla forces are being used in platoon strength.

Eventually the French relinquished their strategic forts on the Chinese frontier, and after the death of General de Lattre de Tassigny (Commander-in-Chief and Civil Governor of French Indo-China from 1950 until his retirement and subsequent death in France in 1952) the tables were turned and in May 1954, after the battle of Dien Bien Phu, the French gave up the fight. They had lost 70000 men, including 2005 officers, the equivalent of five graduating classes of the military academy at St Cyr.

In his introductory letter to *The Quiet American*, Graham Greene says that the book is a story and not a piece of history, and admits to changing the course of events. However, various references – the bombing of Ni Chan, the death of General de Lattre, the references to the war in Korea, the loss of Hao Binh –

seem to indicate that the actions mentioned in the story took place somewhere between 1950–52; Pyle was not yet in Vietnam at the beginning of that period.

At the time when de Lattre was in complete charge, Viet Namh had been constituted as a single state, incorporating Tonkin, Annam and Cochin China, nominally under the rule of the Emperor Bao Dai. It was defended by French forces including the Foreign Legion, parachute and colonial troops, some from North and West Africa. One of these, it is interesting to note, was the self-crowned, recently deposed Emperor Bokassa. All these men were paid in piastres, and the piastre, no matter how much it became devalued, was pegged at the rate of 17 francs; this meant that it could be transferred to Paris and changed into good French money.

The Vietnamese were also helping in the fight against the Vietminh with an ever-increasing regular army and militia. Finally, there were a number of religio-political groups, loosely called 'the sects' who had at one time or another declared themselves the enemies or the friends of the French – and the Vietminh – and who sought to make the best possible deal for themselves. Nor must we forget various aboriginal tribesmen who did not like anybody very much, but if anything preferred the French and their friends.

Of the sects Cao Dai was the strangest. It came into being in the 1920s when a spiritualist seance was addressed by an invisible presence calling himself 'Aaa', who claimed he had been commanded by Cao Dai, the supreme being, to unify the main religions. In 1925 Aaa revealed himself as Cao Dai; his message (like the others written by planchette) was given to Lu Van Trung, a wealthy businessman and a rake. Overnight Lu Van Trung was a reformed character and began the setting up of a temple and religious and temporal state in Taynink (as it is usually spelled). The new religion included saints as diverse as Buddha, Christ, Mahomet, Joan of Arc and Victor Hugo. Cao Dai still sent messages by writing on paper in a jar with a moveable lid (which really acted as a planchette and could give any messages the pope of the sect chose). Women cardinals were allowed because a woman had helped the sect when money was short – she was subsequently made an honorary pope. The sect had an army of sorts, and one of its generals was the defector Thé who helps Pyle in the novel. The

Caodaists were nominally friendly with the French in the period covered by *The Quiet American*. They controlled the rice growing area in Cochin China's Plain of Reeds.

The Hoa-Hao sect was named after the district where the founder had been born. Its members, however, did not believe in temples or elaborate ritual but were very devout. Strongly nationalist, and hence much disliked by the Vietminh, their leader was eventually killed by them. They still had much influence, however, and controlled a large rice growing area in the delta of the Makong River in Cochin China.

Binh Xuyen, though not really a sect, began life as a gang of river pirates, who were believed to have massacred 150 French civilians in one city block in Saigon. The leader of the gang was Bay Vien, who took control of the Grand Monde in the Saigon suburb of Cholon, from whence he organized an empire of prostitution and gambling. Bay Vien sided with the French when he thought that the Vietminh were going to kill him.

The other sect mentioned by Fowler was based in Phat Diem, South Tonkin, where a group of pirates from the Philippine Islands had founded a strong Catholic establishment. Fowler describes it in some detail, so it is enough to say that the archbishop was fanatical and a ruthless disciplinarian. Such was his opposition to the French that, though he took their money, the only white priest in his territory was a Belgian. The French disbanded his army (according to Fowler) when they heard how he was playing them off against the Vietminh.

Pyle is, of course, a complete innocent when confronted with this complicated situation. Whether or not the Economic Aid Committee favoured the Vietminh one cannot be sure, any more than one can be sure that the American OSS had connections with the mission. The Americans at least, believed that the mission was pro-Vietnamese and disliked the 'colonialist' forces of France even though (as Fowler points out) they have something of a colonialist history themselves, in Hawaii for example. The Americans, apart from those at the Aid Mission, did not at first believe that they had a duty to be excessively industrious in equipping the French forces. When the Korean war broke out in 1950 they were glad, however, to have an ally in Vietnam to keep the Communist forces there from becoming engaged on the side of North Korea. There were perhaps some people who believed in York Harding's Third Force, though who would compose it and how it would be employed must have been difficult to decide. Certainly no one in his senses would have chosen General Thé as an ally.

The different sects mentioned, and the French and Vietminh forces, were engaged in a ceaseless struggle for control of the rice crop. Whoever had it controlled the masses of peasants who produced it (yet they themselves were left with the bare minimum). If the French had the rice the Vietminh starved: that was why it was so disastrous for them when they lost Hoabinh, the port on the Black River which threatened the track that joined Ho's northern HQ with the stores of rice and men in Northern Annam. If the French lost it they were regarded with contempt – and still more, with hatred – by the peasants, who then identified themselves with the Vietminh. If any of the sects gained the rice crop they could feed their own armies, deny subsistence to other sects, and trade off the surplus as and when they chose.

The French lost the war, as the Americans lost their Vietnam war, because they could not come to terms with the country or very often get to grips with the enemy. The Vietminh ambushed at will in swamp or jungle – they did not need the sort of road required by mechanized troops; they crossed 'difficult' country while carrying immense loads; they could appear to be harmless peasants by day and then take up their nightly tasks of murder and destruction.

Further reading

The Quicksand War, Lucien Bodard (a friend of Graham Greene) (Faber & Faber).

Viet-Nam Witness (1953–66), Bernard Fall (Pall Mall Press). (This is an excellent series of articles on the early days of the French War.)

A Dragon Apparent, Norman Lewis (Jonathan Cape). (Mainly about Laos and Cambodia.)

There are good sketchmaps and diagrams in the first two books.

Plot and themes

Plot

The plot of *The Quiet American* is relatively straightforward, but the narrative art and detail are almost as complex as the situation in Vietnam itself at the time. The main struggle is between the French and the Vietminh but the various minority movements are simultaneously staging their own wars against the major forces – and each other.

Alden Pyle arrives in Saigon, an earnest and idealistic young American influenced by the writings of a supposed authority on the Far East York Harding. Pyle is seen through the eyes of the narrator, Thomas Fowler, who records events from the personal viewpoint of having as his mistress the girl with whom Pyle falls in love. Constant retrospect by Fowler pin-points the various stages of the plot.

Pyle believes in a Third Force, which will act as a counter-balance to the extremes of Communism on the one hand and French colonialism on the other. He introduces plastic moulds capable of containing explosives and thus of being converted into bombs; Pyle makes contact with the leader of a minority group, General Thé, whom the reader never meets.

Fowler introduces Pyle to Phuong and to her sister, Miss Hei, who shrewdly recognizes Pyle as a man who may offer Phuong the security of marriage. This Fowler cannot do, since his wife stead-fastly refuses to divorce him. Through a series of flashbacks (given here very briefly), the reader is given a resumé of the period leading up to Pyle's murder. Fowler recalls Pyle's confession of his love for Phuong; his own ghastly experiences of war with a French patrol and later in a French aircraft; the first intimations of the bomb with the bicycle explosions; Phuong's desertion after Pyle has saved his life; his (Fowler's) discoveries from Mr Heng of Pyle's activities; and the second terrible explosion (Pyle having failed to realize that a parade had been cancelled) in Saigon at the height of the shopping period.

The horrifying sights Fowler has witnessed in the square send him again to Mr Heng (who works for the Vietminh and is an important contact of Fowler's assistant Dominguez); he agrees to 'talk' to Pyle. In effect, for reasons of personal jealousy and because a pulse of commitment to humanity now beats in him, Fowler has betrayed Pyle. The latter comes to talk to him about Phuong and about the explosion, saying that he has remonstrated with General Thé. Pyle departs, having arranged to meet Fowler later for a meal at the Vieux Moulin: he does not, however, keep the appointment. The reader is now back at the beginning of the story having travelled full circle: it is the night of Pyle's murder and Fowler has returned home to find Phuong waiting in a doorway. Fowler and Phuong are taken to the Sûreté where they are interrogated by Vigot and eventually allowed to return home. A fortnight or so afterwards, Fowler is effectively cleared of suspicion of the murder of Pyle.

On the surface, all ends happily. Fowler's wife writes to say that she has thought things over and will agree to a divorce. Phuong, realizing her sister will be delighted, at this unexpected opportunity of marriage for Phuong, hurries off to see her. Fowler, however, has no one to whom he can make amends for the betrayal: he is aware that in a strange way he cared for Pyle, despite the younger man's dangerous activities and the conventional attitudes which concealed them.

Themes

The themes of the novel are obvious: a hatred of war, of intrigue, an acknowledgement of temptation and jealousy, and the analysis of the battle in a man's consciousness between mere reportage of what is horrible and identification with the human suffering buried beneath the horror. Here the Catholic Greene is in low-key, though Fowler's talk to the priest in Tanyin and his discussions with Pyle and with Vigot all have Catholic elements.

The dilemma of right and wrong is evident: play God, like Pyle, and one must be stopped whatever the cost to the betrayer. Intrigue and deception, whether at press conferences or at higher levels, give place to the overwhelming sense of the degradation of war, with the bodies in the canal and the dying and mutilated in the square living in our memories long after the book is closed.

Structure and style

Structure

The structure of *The Quiet American* is the web of interconnected events which links the past with the present. The first part opens on the night of Pyle's death; the narrator, Thomas Fowler, then defines his relationship with Phuong, before going back in time to his first meeting with Pyle. We learn of the latter's views and of his meeting with Phuong; of the visit by Fowler to Phat Diem and the horrors he witnesses; and of Pyle's visit to him there to confess his love for Phuong.

The second part continues on this personal note, with Pyle asking Phuong to go away with him. The issue is complicated following a visit to Tanyin: Pyle contacts one of General Thé's supporters and later saves Fowler's life after an attack on the watch tower in which they are sheltering. Fowler recovers, returns to Saigon only to hear from his wife that she will not divorce him. He meets Heng via Dominguez and quarrels with Pyle about Phuong.

The plot moves forward in time in the third part. Two weeks after the death of Pyle, Phuong is back living with Fowler, while Vigot continues the murder investigations into the death. Fowler relates the bicycle bomb incident and Phuong's subsequent desertion of him for Pyle. He had gone north, but returned disenchanted and lonely to Saigon. Fowler had previously been offered promotion and a return home, but had rejected it; now he finds the letter awaiting him confirming that he will be staying in Vietnam for at least a year. There follows the terrible explosion in the square.

The final part again returns to the present, with Vigot continuing his investigations. Inevitably this leads Fowler to reflect on the past and his investigations of Pyle. Effectively Fowler betrays him to Heng, who arranges the killing. Fowler keeps the exact details to himself, but Vigot knows the truth. Fowler ends up back with Phuong, freed at last by his wife, but at the same time experiencing the loneliness of regret and conscience.

Style

The Quiet American has twin pivots on which the action turns, and these are facets of style in the broadest sense; they are the use of retrospect, which will be referred to frequently in this Study Aid, and the creation of a convincing atmosphere against which the personal and wider action is played out. The use of a flashback technique is sufficiently covered elsewhere through plot and structure, but atmosphere is endemic in Greene and the locale, whether in Saigon, Phat Diem, Tanyin or a watch tower, is always at the forefront of his presentation. Thus on the very first page of the novel there is the mention of a trishaw, the white silk trousers, the long flowered robe and the first of a number of conversations in a mixture of English and French, the inheritance of the Indo-Chinese just as English is the inheritance of the Chinese in Hong Kong and Singapore.

Note the directness of this atmosphere, which establishes time, place, custom with ease, and with that deft reportage which is so much a mark of Greene's casual yet consummate style. On the memorable night of Pyle's death the atmosphere of snatched love in war 'To take an Annamite to bed with you is like taking a bird: they twitter and sing on your pillow' (12) is balanced by an equally effective escape from the pressures on those who are close to war through their jobs. This kind of escape is epitomized by Phuong's action in 'beating the small paste of opium, twirling her needle', for drugs provide a refuge from the atrocities of war and from the pressures under which civilians suffer in a time of war: witness Monsieur Chou and the number of pipes he smokes in a day. The tightness of the controls exercised is underlined by references to exit permits and orders of circulation, while the heat from which there is no escape is underlined in descriptions like 'A mosquito droned to the attack.'

There is a considered stress on the American nature of the quiet American, with his crew cut (very much the style of the period), his choice of books and his 'unmistakeably young and unused face flung at us like a dart'. This brief quotation in fact summarizes the Greene method, for *The Quiet American* is a figurative novel in the sense that the language is speckled with images of surprising and sudden truth. There are first those redolent of nostalgia: these vary from the relatively innocent 'like a school treat' to the positively ominous 'like the dark passages on upper floors one avoided in childhood': for though the nightmares of childhood are past, the nightmares of the present – senseless and mindless slaughter – will not go away. Thus Fowler's experience in Phat Diem is nowhere more frighteningly endorsed than in the image he chooses to describe the carnage in the canal 'I am reminded now of an Irish stew containing too much meat.' The very homeliness of the association gives the moment a sickening perspective that remains with us. Each body is a human being, or rather was, and Fowler's involvement has begun.

Sometimes the comparisons reflect the quiet order and organization away from it all, for Miss Hei is 'like a chairman with his gavel' or 'He looked like a face on television.' The interested student will find many examples of the range of Greene's figurative style in this novel; perhaps even more impressive are the moments of casual wisdom, phrases and sentences which remain in the mind because of the essential truth they reflect. Take, for example, statements like 'You cannot love without intuition', 'Sometimes she seemed invisible, like peace' or 'He had in his hand the infinite riches of respectability.' Frequently of course these statements are reinforced by imagery, by apt comparisons and associations which extend their own validity 'Silence like a plant put out tendrils' and 'carrying Fate in the lines of their faces as others on the palm'.

But if Greene writes with imagination and figurative force, he also has a wealth of wisdom on which to base his assertions. He and Vigot quote Pascal, an Indo-Chinese official is interested in Wordsworth, and Fowler's threatened recall to England causes him to remark inwardly 'Dante never thought up that turn of the screw for his condemned lovers. Paolo was never promoted to Purgatory.' At another time Fowler quotes Baudelaire, and there are many other quotations which indicate a wealth of reading on Greene's part. There is too an insistent commentary of wider reference – the political heads of state from Eisenhower through Ho Chi Minh to Sun Yat Sen to de Gaulle to de Lattre, so that a broad atmosphere of realism is created. Because Fowler is the narrator, this is often given an ironic tone; Fowler is not only jealous of Pyle, he is also extremely satirical about the American way of life 'We used to speak of sterling qualities. Have we got to talk now about a dollar love?'. This satire sometimes takes the form of parody, as when Granger gives a mock account of a telegram:

Great victory north-west of Hanoi. French recapture two villages they never told us they'd lost. Heavy Vietminh casualties. Haven't been able to count their own yet but will let us know in a week or two.

This moves from the formal to the laconic, the style exactly reflecting the hopelessness of ever discovering the truth.

Part of Greene's style is deliberately colloquial, as in the conversations between Vigot and Fowler, and for him dialogue is character, from the sometimes cynical irony of Fowler to the cliché-ridden conventionalities of Pyle 'You have to fight for liberty'. No word is wasted, and again one is forced to admire the exactness of description which can bring a scene alive. Greene, as we have said, is a strongly visual writer:

Across the way a *métisse* with long and lovely legs lay coiled after her smoke reading a glossy woman's paper, and in the cubicle next to her two middle-aged Chinese transacted business, sipping tea, their pipes laid aside. (Part 3, Chapter 1, p.151)

This is the eye for detail, but the eye for realism and the spiritual associations of death and destruction is even more sure, even more graphic both in terms of the scene and the observer's comment inlaid in an uncompromising directness of language:

A woman sat on the ground with what was left of her baby in her lap; with a kind of modesty she had covered it with her straw peasant hat. She was still and silent, and what struck me most in the square was the silence. It was like a church I had once visited during Mass ... The legless torso at the edge of the garden still twitched, like a chicken which has lost its head. (Part 3, Chapter 2, p.162)

We have given these extracts in some fullness because they indicate the variety of Greene's powers. It is not enough to claim that he is a camera – as Fowler claims he is merely a reporter – for cameras cannot have feelings, and Greene's writing is imbued with feeling for suffering, frail, vulnerable humanity. The narrative tension is maintained by switches of focus until all the pieces in what is a kind of moving jigsaw are fitted together. The adhesive is irony (but with compassion), figurative vividness (nearly always appropriate and moving), a mastery of the colloquial and the realistic, and a kind of in-built moral commentary which gives perspective to events.

The use of the first-person narrator is also a triumph, for the revelations of Fowler's consciousness constitute the mainstream of the action. The ironic mode of his own expression is qualified even at the end – with marriage before him he has to live with betrayal and regret, with a past which has removed him from the *dégagé* to the *engagé* but which may still leave him a wanderer, unwilling to return to the desk being kept warm for him. But the horror of man's bestiality to man is very strong upon him, and that which corrupted Kurz in *Heart of Darkness* has corrupted Pyle in *The Quiet American*. And just as the river in Conrad's remarkable story is symbolic of the twistings and turnings of corruption and justification, so the Christian/Unitarian Pyle has learned – in the words that typify Greene's style in this novel, and which Fowler uses to Dominguez – 'from Nero how to make human bodies into candles'.

In *The Quiet American* we see the journalistic elevated to the literary and the literary containing that sense of the particular and the general in humanitarian concern and compassion which is the hallmark of a great writer.

Characters

Thomas Fowler

a man of middle age, with eyes a little bloodshot, beginning to put on
weight, ungraceful in love, less noisy than Granger perhaps but more
cynical, less innocent

'I'm not involved', I repeated. It had been an article of my creed. The
human condition being what it was, let them fight, let them love, let
them murder, I would not be involved ... I wrote what I saw: I took
no action – even an opinion is a kind of action.

The two quotations given above outline the appearance of Fowler
and what he believes to be his character. The first-person narrator
is conscious of his age (he stresses always that Pyle is younger and
stronger) and conscious too that his job is to report objectively the
events he sees and the situations in which he finds himself. But
just as in life he has separated from his wife and left a previous
mistress called Anne, so Fowler departs in himself from his own conception of what he is. Yet throughout he plays dangerously for the
visit to Phat Diem signals the beginning of his involvement and the
later explosion in the square at Saigon confirms it. It causes him to
betray Pyle to Mr Heng, though he nearly has second thoughts on
this. Fowler is a wanderer on the face of the earth, dreading the
ties of home though experiencing considerable nostalgia for them.

The fear of being emotionally involved dogs him, yet the thought
of losing Phuong to Pyle brings out a savage side to his character,
seen in the violence of his love-making and his determined devalua-
tion of everything American. Ironically, Phuong has really made
few demands on him, and the imagery Fowler uses of her is light
and ephemeral, like the passage of a bird or butterfly. This confirms
to the reader that her role – opium-mixer and personless yielder to
the 'formula' of love-making – is a role undertaken on his terms,
for Phuong has given up the respectability her sister so wants for her
in order to live with Fowler. The latter is, however, vulnerable, as
the arrival of Pyle shows; he is moved to jealousy and to cynicism
when Pyle declares his love for Phuong, but he behaves – initially at
least – reasonably in Phat Diem when Pyle comes to tell him of that
love.

And here we note an important facet of Fowler's character, for he reacts to the horrific aspects of war as we should expect any humanitarian to react: far from Phuong in Phat Diem, he can talk rationally with Pyle to cover the inward wound made by his experiences in the body-filled canal. The action of Fowler's consciousness as narrator is to move backwards into the past. Thus his reportage to us the readers is the record of Fowler in interaction with Phuong, with Pyle, with Granger, or talking Pascal and manoeuvring with Vigot, weighing the significance of what Heng shows him, and reasoning with Trouin about the seemingly casual shooting up of the sampan. Fowler has moments of acute failure and humiliation, for example his inability to make love to the *métisse*, and his dependence on Pyle after the bazooka attack on the watch tower. Fowler is a lonely man, driven in upon himself by his past and the fear of being hurt attendant on commitment. But he is nothing less than human, even lying to Pyle about his wife's intention to divorce him.

In any novel, the difficulty in analysing the first-person narrator is that one runs the risk of identifying the author with his creation, and there are clearly times when Greene is using his reporter/observer Fowler as a mouthpiece. In narration of this kind, however, we must look closely at what Fowler says in the context of his relationship with Phuong and his attitudes towards the war he is reporting. He is nostalgic and cynical at the same time, as we have seen, but he sees through Pyle, or perhaps more correctly through the pretentiousness of York Harding. He speaks his mind after Pyle's death, knowing in his heart that he is at least partly responsible for that death. But Fowler blames it on the way the Americans handle their aid programmes, where a false ideology has been allowed to overcome rational appraisal:

He had no more of a notion than any of you what the whole affair's about, and you gave him money and York Harding's books on the East and said 'Go ahead. Win the East for democracy.' (Part 1, Chapter 2, p.32)

Indeed, when we are considering Fowler, we should perhaps remember Greene's cautionary remark in the dedication of the novel to Réné and Phuong – 'This is a story and not a piece of history.' In the context of the story Fowler is central and crucial, for everything is seen through his eyes, felt through his senses, subjected to his judgement. From the very beginning of the novel, we sense

Fowler's guilt over Pyle 'I couldn't stay quiet any longer', but even here he recalls how much he has suffered from Pyle's opinionated behaviour. We see his weakness, his need to get away from a situation in part of his own making, when he inhales the pipe that Phuong has prepared.

Fowler is quite strong-willed though, refusing to let Vigot interrogate Phuong unless he too is present. He is also something of an actor, for although he half-suspects what has happened to Pyle, he sustains the idea in Vigot's mind that Pyle is going to marry Phuong. Fowler also knows himself, aware that when he leaves Saigon he will feel nostalgia for the sight of the girls walking through the streets. He realizes too the effect that the opium has on him: it makes him feel less guilty, and helps him to the reasonable assertion that Pyle always went his own way. When he learns of Pyle's death, Fowler is quick to explain that he got mixed up, but in effect he shows his own clear-sightedness of what Pyle should have done 'He belonged to the skyscraper and the express-elevator.'

Even before he gets to know Pyle, Fowler is strongly anti-American; he at first admires Pyle's loyalty to York Harding and willingly explains the situation in Indo-China to him. Fowler first realizes how potentially dangerous Pyle is when the 'Third Force' is mentioned: he immediately equates it with other similarly fanatic groups such as the Fifth Column and Seventh Day Adventists. When Vigot is searching through Pyle's belongings, Fowler is astute enough to take with him York Harding's *The Rôle of The West*, almost as if he is protecting the dead man from the discovery of his own motives. Perhaps it is his way of showing that he cares for him. Fowler's conversation with the Economic Attaché indicates that he has no time for hypocrisy and dissembling, for he despises the words 'died a soldier's death in cause of Democracy'.

Yet Fowler's reactions towards Pyle when he was alive were curiously mixed. Remember the way he protected him, for instance with Granger, getting him away from the latter in the House of the Five Hundred Girls. Fowler is a cynic with a razor edged sense of humour, see his wry definition of American aid as 'electrical sewing machines for starving seamstresses' to the literal Miss Hei. He enjoys teasing Pyle and, of course, shocking him too, but Fowler is a good reporter, who goes north to the really unpleasant action because that is what his duty demands. He is observant, courageous (though perhaps not in his own mind) and impartial insofar as he can be; however, the canal experience and the sight of the dead child erode his determination about his own distance from it all. Fowler is committed now because of his feelings 'I hate war', though at this stage he does not realize the movement within himself.

Fowler is strangely tolerant when Pyle arrives unexpectedly to announce his love for Phuong, and obviously the recent experiences in Phat Diem have helped to make him so. He realizes, only too clearly, the advantages of youth, respectability and marriageability which Pyle possesses in the coming battle for Phuong. He is irritated enough to be crudely honest – 'You can have her interests. I only want her body. I want her in bed with me.' Fowler's reaction to the news of his promotion is equally predictable; it elevates his feelings for the rue Catinat, creates a nostalgia for the present, so that he cannot think of England as 'Home'. Just as he has given himself up to a kind of inverted nostalgia for the London of far away, so now he feels only contempt for the night-editor and 'his semi-detached villa at Streatham'.

This mood is succeeded by one of Pyle-baiting; this he pushes to the utmost in Phuong's presence, so that Pyle asks her to go away with him. Her 'No' brings an 'enormous relief' to Fowler, and sets him off on the quest for freedom from his wife back at 'home'. The visit to Tanyin finds Fowler reflective, enigmatically so, pondering on religion and the force of his memories. It is this mood which perhaps makes him only half-aware of Pyle and the commandant and the fact that nothing has apparently been done to Pyle's car. It also makes him forget to check his own car. When they arrive at the watch tower Fowler experiences a moment of fear; this is followed by a further discussion with Pyle, where Fowler's intuition that Pyle is misguided, causes him to engage in some cynical repartee despite the seriousness of the issues at stake 'A lot of energy with your people seems to go into whistling' and 'It's not in the Kinsey report.' This flippancy conceals his concern over Pyle's possible success with Phuong, and there is a distinct pathos as he considers his own coming 'old age and death. I wake up with these in mind and not a woman's body. I just don't want to be alone in my last decade.' Even when he is wounded Fowler thinks of one of the guards in the watch tower as 'like a child who is frightened of the dark and yet afraid to scream'. This image haunts him through his pain until he is given an injection of morphia, for 'I was responsible for that voice crying in the dark.'

When Fowler's wife sends her first reply to his letter he learns 'how open the sexual wounds remain over the years'. We sense that Fowler has gone, over a period of time, from woman to woman, but he is deeply moved and hurt by his wife's pain and, one supposes, by his own sense of guilt. This does not prevent him, insecure and vulnerable as he is, from writing the lie to Pyle. Fowler is persistent, following through Dominguez's hints about Pyle until he finds what he wants – the implication that Pyle is not merely a passive idealist but a wrongly committed one as well. This presents something of a dilemma for Fowler; Pyle has saved his life yet Fowler knows that Pyle is wrongly committed and that he is capable of inflicting suffering on others. Fowler's reference to Pyle as 'my saviour' is therefore tinged with irony, the wry recognition of the dual attitude he has towards the quiet American.

Fowler is also something of an intellectual, able to quote Pascal in a kind of mental *Quatre Cent Vingt-et-un* with Vigot 'But he who chooses heads and he who chooses tails are equally at fault.' However, perhaps the most poignant moments in Fowler's life are when he is alone and uncertain about Phuong's intentions; these moments are crystallized when he wakes and finds the pillow undented and Phuong gone. Later, after the visit to Pyle, Fowler breaks down, capable, as we see, of emotion in his private life yet able to resist emotional involvement *vis-à-vis* his fellow beings in the theatre of war. His conscience, however, pushes him on into these wider affairs, and he is made more bitter by the shooting of the sampan. It strengthens his feelings of compassion and he is later kinder to Pyle than he thought was possible. But reaction to the explosion forces his hand. Fowler sees Pyle as 'impregnably armoured by his good intentions' and concludes that 'Innocence is a kind of insanity.' He betrays him, almost reneges on the betrayal, and escapes again with Phuong, knowing himself to be guilty yet having no one to whom he can confess his remorse.

Fowler, in essence, is each and all of us, capable of error but capable too of a compassion for the mass of humanity which tells him that the demagogue who uses the materials of war is culpable and evil. He conceals from Vigot the fact that he did see Pyle the night he died, but perhaps more important than this is his response to Granger, whom he initially disliked. Fowler is sympathetic about his son, and even offers to do his story for him. Perhaps this private manifestation of his capacity for love is pathetic too, for even with Phuong back he is a lonely man, an 'isolationist too' as he once confessed to Pyle.

Alden Pyle

an unmistakeably young and unused face flung at us like a dart. With his gangly legs and his crew-cut and his wide campus gaze he seemed incapable of harm.

There is an element of surprise when the reader learns that Alden Pyle is thirty two years old. Despite his reading, the knowledge he has gained through York Harding and his earnestness, Pyle seems younger, perhaps one of life's permanent innocents. The extract above however contains the innuendo of his deception: 'Look like the innocent flower/But be the serpent under it' counsels Lady Macbeth of her husband – and this is Pyle's stance, though without the self-awareness of wrong-doing which Lord and Lady Macbeth possess and which brings them both to death through murder and madness. The last two words have been chosen deliberately because this is what the ignorance (and innocence) of Pyle brings about. Pyle is a dangerous man, imbued with the idea of the Third Force, acting in the name of democracy against his twin hates of colonialism (here the French) and Communism. As a result, Pyle intrigues with General Thé, and imports moulds (for bicycle pumps) into the country as these make effective containers for explosives. But the name of the game is war and suffering, and Pyle does not face up to these harsh realities until he stands in the square with the blood soaking his shoes. Even here he lays the blame elsewhere (while thinking of having his shoes cleaned) 'they shouldn't have cancelled the parade, it must have been the Communists.' The contempt the reader feels for him far exceeds the anger expressed by Fowler. Later Pyle tells how he has reprimanded General Thé, but we know, as does Fowler, that he has no conception of war or of the corruption it brings in its wake.

Pyle is the all-American boy from the right kind of background; he is a university graduate whose study and appreciation of the complexities of politics in the East are based on the misguided opinions of a third-rate journalistic hack. Though he has spent but a few months in the East (compared to Fowler's years of experience), Pyle thinks that he has all the answers. In effect he has none, and is totally ignorant of the chaos he creates. The implication here is that decency and respectability are skin-deep and for this reason Greene makes a penetrating study of the character of Pyle.

Easily shocked and embarrassed, dancing at arm's length with somebody else's mistress, buying a boat to get to Phat Diem to confess to Fowler his love for Phuong, Pyle is intent on doing the right thing, and relieved when Fowler's response is more reasonable than he had been led to expect. Admittedly he does respond to Fowler's baiting and asks Phuong to go away with him, but prior to this he has held forth on Phuong's need for children and a settled life. Again his immaturity is apparent, and one wonders if his love for Phuong is a part of his determined democracy; whether he sees in their union the meeting of East and West which his ideology and practical action covet.

But Pyle is a minnow among tritons, a quiet American whose errors of ideology are mirrored in his errors of execution. He is easily found out by Mr Heng, easily traced by Fowler in his search for clues, easily misled and betrayed by Fowler to his death. However, Pyle is responsible for a frightful escalation in human suffering from the joke of the bicycle bomb to the explosion in the square, and just as his appearance has belied the power he innocently wields, so the cover-up after his death is equally superficial, misleading and dishonest. Pyle has not died a hero's death, though his parents will think he has, and that the secret operations were important. They were, but not, as Pyle perhaps believed, to the cause of peace – they were symptomatic of and subservient to the cause of war – mindless, with common sense offered as an excuse for a degraded and inexcusable assertion of power.

Phuong

I couldn't see her face, only the white silk trousers and the long flowered robe, but I knew her for all that. She had so often waited for me to come home at just this place and hour.

Phuong, Fowler's Annamite mistress, is from a good mandarin family and has a possessive and influential older sister Miss Hei, who is intent on respectability for Phuong; by this Miss Hei means a good marriage, preferably with a European or an American or a settlement. She therefore disapproves of Fowler who can neither marry nor afford a settlement.

The imagery used to describe Phuong is bird imagery: lightness, the ease of coming and going, marking a certain impersonality; for the core of Phuong, should she have one, remains a mystery. She is the typical Eastern girl, subservient to the male, making his opium pipe with great care and deliberation, responding obediently to Fowler's sexual needs and being shunted between the two men with no apparent display of emotion. Phuong accepts Pyle's death quietly, never speaks of him or advances an opinion; she moves back in with Fowler just as unassertively as she moved out.

In fact we know little of Phuong; we know that Fowler met her when she was a dancer, and we also know that it took him some four months to persuade her to live with him. She speaks in French, having acquired no or very little English since she has lived with Fowler. Only twice in the novel does Phuong display any positive response to the intimate events which surround her. The first occasion is when she says that she will not go to live with Pyle, and the second is at the very end of the novel when she races off to tell her sister that she is going to be the second 'Mrs Fowlair'. Her one passion in life is for films, which provide a temporary refuge from the commonplace of living.

Fowler of course understands what Phuong's exterior conceals – or at least he thinks he does: here she is after Pyle's death – 'There was no scene, no tears, just thought – the long private thought of somebody who has to alter a whole course of life.' Yet no one would know. Phuong is obviously very attractive, for Granger admires her even in his inebriated state; she clearly has an air of innocence despite her life with Fowler, which endears her to Pyle. There is every suggestion that she is under her sister's thumb or rather hand for Miss Hei clamps it down on Phuong's knee on one occasion to register her authority. Moreover Phuong is proud of this sister who, according to her, was once in business in Singapore.

But for all this – her beauty, her beautiful dancing, Phuong is nebulous in terms of personality; as Fowler puts it, 'Sometimes she seemed invisible, like peace.' And of course for Fowler she is peace, the peace of the pipe, the peace of undemanding sexuality, the peace of the third person he often feels her to be – the shield against the past and the comfort of the present.

Vigot

he appeared incongruously in love with his wife, who ignored him, a flashy and false blonde . . . and he had a volume of Pascal open on his desk to while away the time

Vigot is the French officer at the Sûreté, quiet, intellectual, tired and depressed. He is apologetic to Fowler for having to interrogate him, and establishes with Fowler a kind of understanding. He affects to suspect him, but is sharp enough to notice details, though he is rather caught off balance when Fowler abruptly asks if Pyle is in the mortuary. He is honest enough to admit that he is not altogether sorry that Pyle is dead, and realistic, as he demonstrates by the quick and efficient examination of Pyle and the finding of mud in his lungs.

The day after Pyle's death finds Vigot going through his things, pondering on whether or not this is a simple case of jealousy. He allows Fowler to take Phuong's things from Pyle's apartment, and he also lets him take York Harding's *The Rôle of the West*. Vigot is anxious to find out as much as he can, but admits 'My report's all tied up. He was murdered by the Communists. Perhaps the beginning of a campaign against American aid.' There is a kind of sadness about Vigot, for he is a thinker and perhaps a philosopher who finds himself doing a particular job. Perhaps too his wife's infidelities bulk large in his mind.

Later Vigot comes to see Fowler to tell him that he now knows that Fowler has lied – that in fact he did see Pyle on the night he died. The thoroughness of his investigations can be seen in this checking of the smallest details. He is scrupulously fair though, and tells Fowler that he doesn't intend to bother him any more.

Granger

Bill Granger – you can't keep him out of a scrap

At first Granger is an unattractive character, drunk, brash, evincing what Fowler calls 'Rough soldierly manners'. He is after 'a piece of tail', obviously enjoys a trishaw race, speaks in colloquialisms and petty obscenities and has a coarse sense of humour. Granger also has a shrewd sense of humour, however, as can be seen in his parody of a French press statement; he gives an accurate account of what happens and of how press conferences are really a form of farce. Fowler is closer to him than he realizes, for it is Granger who penetrates the French press conference and establishes that, in terms of military aid, the American commitment is feeble and non-productive.

Granger distributes his money and manhood in the House of the Five Hundred Girls, but the final meeting with him reveals that under this vulgar exterior there is more to him; he too has a capacity for suffering. He speaks his mind bluntly to Fowler and tells him that his (Granger's) son has got polio. There is a terrible pathos in the fact that Granger does not believe in God, and he appreciates the sympathy Pyle gives him, while acknowledging that they are 'cat and dog'. We are particularly touched by the fact that although he is suffering himself, his thoughts are for his wife, who 'can't drink, can she?'. In all, Granger is a much more sympathetic character than we are led to believe at first.

Minor characters

We have already mentioned *Miss Hei*, the older sister who determines that Phuong will achieve a respectable marriage. She has no sense of humour, but knows that her sister's beauty is a commercial asset. Miss Hei encourages Phuong in her conquest of Pyle, and interrogates Fowler about Pyle's parents and prospects. The *Economic Attaché* is a bore and a dishonest one at that, who covers up for Pyle and asserts that he has died a hero's death. He is of course annoyed with Fowler, who informs him in no uncertain terms that he, his kind and York Harding are responsible for the death of Pyle. The Economic Attaché's shallowness is shown however when Phuong is mentioned; he is even grateful to Fowler for having tried to prevent the match between Phuong and Pyle, which would have been something of an embarrassment to this pretentious arch-democrat. *Trouin* is typical, a realist in terms of the war and in terms of life, who shoots up the sampan because it *might* be acting for the enemy. He offers Fowler the *métisse*, whom he and another airman have already had.

All the characters contribute to the realism of *The Quiet American*, from the first entrance of the man from the Sûreté to pick up Fowler, through Fowler's experience with the French patrol in Phat Diem to individuals seen silently in time of stress, like the fat little priest scurrying past with something under a napkin. Greene has the authentic touch, and character exists for him, and hence for us, in verbal and visual clarity of presence.

Chapter summaries and textual notes

Part one
Chapter 1

The narrator, whom we later come to know as Fowler, tells of the night in February when he waited in his room for the 'quiet American' Pyle to return. Fowler's ex-mistress Phuong was also waiting to see Pyle in the next doorway and he had invited her in to reminisce. Phuong had changed since becoming Pyle's girl and Fowler noted every change. Later in the evening Phuong had made him an opium pipe and had told him of the plans Pyle had made to marry her. Fowler had asked Phuong to spend the night with him as he was sure that Pyle would not now come.

They had been interrupted by a knock at the door and were surprised to find a member of the Sûreté there requesting that they accompany him to the station. Phuong was interrogated by Vigot who also questioned Fowler on his – and Pyle's – relationship with the girl. Fowler was asked about his first meeting with Pyle (which he recalled silently to himself); he asked Vigot if Pyle was in the mortuary much to the inspector's surprise. After Fowler had provided an alibi for his whereabouts that evening, Vigot revealed that Pyle had been found dead 'in the water under the bridge to Dakow'. Fowler accompanied Vigot to the mortuary to identify the body only too aware that he was a prime suspect (the motive: jealousy over Phuong switching her affections to Pyle). Fowler took Phuong home and told her the news of Pyle's death: she remained the night apparently unmoved and Fowler was left to wonder if he had been the only one to care for Pyle.

Greene moves from the present to the past with some rapidity, and for this reason the events detailed in this chapter have all been put into the past tense; in fact the novel does come full circle.

rue (Fr.) street.
black trousers Traditional Chinese dress for women, made of light material.

trishaw i.e. a combination of tricycle and rickshaw, in effect a large tricycle pedalled by one man and taking one or at most two passengers.

small courtesies i.e. being considerate and polite about minor matters.

Phoenix The mythical bird which rises again from its ashes, (see next line of the text).

Je sais ... la fenêtre (Fr.) I know. I saw you alone at the window.

Tu es troublé (Fr.) you are worried.

a mandarin A Chinese official – Phuong still has some class-awareness. Phuong, however, was Annamite (see below).

pronounced i.e. definite.

Hitler Adolf Hitler (1889–1945) the German leader who came to power early in the 1930s, the founder of Nazism who precipitated the Second World War by invading Poland in 1939. All available evidence suggests that he and his wife committed suicide in his bunker in Berlin in 1945.

Princess Margaret The sister of the present Queen Elizabeth, Princess Margaret was born in 1930.

Annamite A native of Annam, the central province of French Indo-China as it then was. (See the section on 'Background').

even from France The implication is that France is home for the Colonials in this area, just as England would be home for anyone English in India at this time.

like a convolvulus reversed Note the economy of the style and the explicitness of the image – a convolvulus is a kind of twining plant (also called bindweed) with white, trumpet-shaped flowers.

pulls i.e. drags, inhalations.

Baudelaire's Charles Baudelaire (1821–67) French symbolist poet whose most important work was *Les Fleurs du Mal*.

Mon enfant, ma soeur This is from Baudelaire's *L'Invitation Au Voyage*, and the lines mean: My child, my sister (then Fowler misses out two lines) to love as we choose, to love and to die in the land which is the image of you.

dont l'humeur est vagabonde This line occurs later in the same poem and means the ships are nomadic by inclination, by choice.

indigenous i.e. native, with special reference to flora and fauna.

Sureté More correctly spelt *Sûreté*, this is the headquarters of the French detective police force (akin to our CID).

Toi aussi (Fr.) you too.

Say vous In any form of address, French makes a distinction between the polite form (*vous*) and the familiar form (*tu*). Fowler is reprimanding the policeman for addressing Phuong in such familiar terms.

Sur le chung i.e. at once, immediately; a mispronunciation of *sur le champ* (Fr.).

order of circulation i.e. freedom to move about in the country.

exit permit i.e. permission to leave (the country).

Saigon The capital of French Indo-China.

Hoa-Haos ... Caodaists ... General Thé See section on 'Background'.

Pascal Blaise Pascal (1623–62) the illustrious French thinker and writer. *Les Pensées* were published after his death.

Economic Aid Mission Part of the American Aid Programme after the Second World War.

A mosquito droned to the attack At once suggestive of atmosphere and of the aerial attacks mentioned later in the novel.

crew-cut Fashionable hairstyle for men of the time – cropped, very short hair.

campus i.e. suggestive of college life.

staled i.e. grown stale or commonplace.

they never made the European Press i.e. mention of these small-scale incidents was never reported where it counts – in Europe.

Congress The national legislative body of the United States of America.

You cannot love without intuition Note the economy and the truth behind this comment.

youth and hope ... age and despair Typical of Greene's antithetical style.

Dakow A riverside suburb of Saigon.

Vietminh See section on 'Background'.

Yankee An American, strictly an inhabitant of New England.

American Legation i.e. the diplomatic centre. Most countries have legations in other countries, particularly the major ones.

The wounds were frozen into placidity A superb contrast with the violence which caused them.

Comment? (Fr.) What?

the Middle Ages About AD 1000–1400. This is the first of the references to the Middle Ages which point to the ancient as well as the modern nature of society in Indo-China.

dude-ranch i.e. for people who could afford to pay to play at being cowboys.

Long Island The island situated in south-east New York is 185 km (118 miles) long, 20 to 32 km (12 to 20 miles) wide.

One has to in this climate i.e. because the flesh would quickly turn putrid in the heat.

the vanity of the cuckold Fowler feels that he has been usurped by Pyle in Phuong's affections (i.e. made a cuckold of) but Pyle is now dead.

censors i.e. those employed to censure anything from the news reports which was considered politically undesirable.

a Paris date-line i.e. when it was released in Paris.

Sa douce langue natale This is the final line of the second verse of Baudelaire's poem *L'Invitation Au Voyage* (referred to earlier) 'Your gentle native speech'.

Il est mort (Fr.) he is dead.

Tu dis? (Fr.) what did you say?

Assassiné (Fr.) murdered.

Chapter 2

Section 1

Here we have the author using a technique similar to the flashback device much exploited in films. Greene is consciously integrating past and present. Fowler thinks back to his first meeting with Pyle. Pyle had struck him as a quiet, modest, idealistic young man much influenced by the writer York Harding. Though Fowler attempted to explain the complexity of the situation in Vietnam, Pyle cut through all this, saying that he believed, as did York Harding, in the necessity of a 'Third Force' for the East. This was the first pointer to the obsession by which Pyle allowed himself to be governed and which later dominates the plot. Greene will unfold the plot of the novel through these retrospective sequences. Though Fowler makes no mention of the fact to Pyle at the time, he is living with his Annamite mistress Phuong.

Section 2

The reader is now returned to the present – in fact the morning after Pyle's death. Fowler goes to the dead man's apartment to collect Phuong's belongings and there meets Vigot. The latter has already made a thorough search of the place and more particularly of Pyle's possessions. With Vigot's acquiescence, Fowler takes York Harding's *The Rôle of the West* as a keepsake.

On leaving the building, Fowler meets the American Economic Attaché who conveys the Minister's concern over the news of Pyle's death. We learn that Pyle's father is an expert on underwater erosion. Fowler is only angered by the Attaché's comments and the cover-up operation which is being instigated. As far as he is concerned, Pyle is an innocent who failed to understand the complexities of the situation in Vietnam and as such paid the price.

Textual notes, Sections 1–2

sour cracks i.e. bitter remarks or jokes.

Hanoi See section on 'Background'.

like a school-treat Note the homeliness of the image, which contrasts effectively with the terrible reality of the fighting.

the terrace i.e. because it is higher up.

York Harding An ingenious combination of the legendary American soldier Sergeant York and a famous American President.

Guerlain perfume i.e. from the exclusive French perfumery house of Guerlain. Fowler finds comfort in items such as these which remind him that Saigon is not so far removed from western civilization.

distant thirty hours i.e. by air.

The Advance of Red China Title, typical of its kind, calculated to prey on American public feeling against and fear of Communism.

straight stuff i.e. real history.

brief me i.e. fill me in, give me the main points.

denigrations i.e. their cynicism.

Tonkin ... Red River ... Haiphong See section on 'Background'.

watch towers These are sufficiently defined later in the novel – they are in effect elevated guardhouses which command a view of the flat terrain.

Binh Xuyen See section on 'Background'.

Fifth Column, Third Force, Seventh Day The first is the force within a country which sympathizes with and organizes the way for the coming invaders, while the Seventh Day Adventists are an extreme religious cult. Fowler equates Pyle's Third Force with these two fanatic groups.

mollusc i.e. the shell-like shape of the hats.

Bloomsbury square ... Euston ... Torrington Place Fowler's nostalgia takes him back to the celebrated West End square associated with Virginia Woolf, to Euston Station and to Torrington Place which runs between Tottenham Court Road and Gower Street and is situated close to London University.

Foreign Legion i.e. the French Foreign Legion, which enlisted soldiers of all nationalities.

képis French military caps with horizontal peaks.

epaulettes Ornamental shoulder-pieces on the uniforms.

like the dark passages And, ironically, Vietnam carries its own fears.

Tabu i.e. forbidden, a good name for a dirty magazine.

her elevenses Fowler's mood of nostalgia causes him to use this phrase, which is peculiarly English.

Grand Monde A common name for a place of entertainment in the Far East.

croissants Crescent-shaped bread rolls.

de Gaulle ... Leclerc ... de Lattre Charles de Gaulle (1890–1970) from his exile in London, led the French resistance against Germany during the Second World War. He became the first President of France's Fifth Republic in 1958. Philippe Leclerc (1902–47) was Commander-in-Chief of the French forces in Indo-China in 1945, was relieved of his post in 1946 and died the following year. For de Lattre see section on 'Background'.

making passes at the General's concubines i.e. flirting with them.

like a butterfly in a room A light image, which one would associate with the character of Phuong anyway.

Lecoq ... Maigret The first was the creation of Emile Gaboriau (1823–73) the father of French detective fiction; Maigret is the legendary French detective in the crime fiction of Georges Simenon.

Congressional i.e. the results of particular investigations in the United States.

War in the Philippines Possibly a reference to the American acquisition of the islands to the north of the Malay Archipelago from Spain in the war of 1898.

Thomas Wolfe (1900–38) American writer who had considerable influence on his contemporaries.

The Triumph of Life An inflated, pretentious title.

The Physiology of Marriage Again, a fairly commonplace title, whether scientifically researched or written by an individual crank is not clear.

vermouth cassis Vermouth is a white wine flavoured with wormwood, and cassis is a rather syrupy blackcurrant flavouring for drinks. This drink is clearly a mixture of the two.

big bang i.e. an explosion.

Merde (Fr.) shit – an expletive expressive here of frustration and impatience.

Packard Large American car, suitable as a staff car for diplomats.

darned Polite form of 'damned'.

President Presumably of Indo-China, Vietnam.

underwater erosion Even here there is irony, for the above-water erosion is caused by man and his wars.

Time Celebrated American magazine with an international circulation.

Purple Hearts American decoration for those wounded in action.
hunch i.e. guess, idea.
A Red menace, a soldier of democracy i.e. Pyle couldn't tell the
  difference, but the narrator is of the opinion that there is no
  difference.
the Book Club i.e. producing cheap editions for a wider readership
  of potential best-sellers.

Chapter 3

Section 1

Greene again uses the flashback technique though this time to
describe Pyle's first meeting with Phuong. Fowler and Phuong were
at the Continental and had been invited by Pyle to join his table.
They found themselves seated next to the Economic Attaché and a
man called Granger who had just won a trishaw race against a
drunken Frenchman. Granger was both loud and coarse and
declared his desire for a girl for the night while at the same time
holding forth on the state of the war in Vietnam. Pyle clearly dis-
approved of his drunken behaviour and his sexual innuendoes, some
of which inevitably embraced Phuong. Pyle and Granger had later
gone on to the House of the Five Hundred Girls from which Fowler
succeeded in retrieving Pyle; however, Granger was left, surrounded
by money-scavenging girls, much to the latter's delight. Pyle had
been clearly upset by the pretty girls: their innocent looks were
clearly not in keeping with their corrupted natures.

Section 2

Pyle and Fowler joined Phuong at the Chalet: Fowler fleetingly sees
himself as 'a man of middle-age, with eyes a little bloodshot,
beginning to put on weight'. Greene now employs a flashback
within a flashback as Fowler ponders on his early courtship of
Phuong. While she and Pyle are dancing, Fowler is joined by Miss
Hei, Phuong's elder sister. Anxious to help her younger sister
towards a good marriage, she questions Fowler on Pyle. Later in
talking to Pyle, Miss Hei adopts a tone which is calculated to draw
him in the direction of marriage – e.g. how nice it would be for

his parents to have grandchildren of their own. Fowler watched them dance together again, and realized how much he loved Phuong. Fowler, however, is essentially a realist, and was aware even then that Phuong would leave him sometime. Afterwards they watched the cabaret, and in particular the group of female impersonators who were performing that evening.

Textual notes, Sections 1–2

Quatre Cent Vingt-et-un As is indicated here, a game played with dice, for money.

Economic Attaché i.e. a diplomat, in this case probably responsible for the dispensing of economic aid.

right deodorants A wry comment on the (supposed) fanatical American attitude towards personal hygiene, and the advertising empire behind it.

war horses See Job, 39,25.

the Sporting i.e. a club.

a photo-finish Again note the irony inherent in the term.

Didn't know you had a whistle in you A reference to the 'wolf-whistling' after girls practised by Americans everywhere in wartime – but it also means that he didn't appreciate the attractions of the Economic Attaché.

can American slang for lavatory.

U.P. United Press.

Thank God for penicillin i.e. because it is the standard, effective treatment for venereal disease.

The Frogs can't take Scotch i.e. the French can't drink whisky.

Ordre de Circulation i.e. a permit granting freedom of movement.

file i.e. place, give.

Road 66 . . . Highway to Hell The road was used by the French for moving troops and supplies and was therefore frequently the target of ambushes, hence its name 'Highway to Hell'.

Pulitzer An annual award for achievements in American journalism, literature.

Stephen Crane (1870–1900) American writer whose book on the American Civil War became a classic of its kind; it was entitled *The Red Badge of Courage*.

all this shop i.e. talk, gossip which is over familiar.

Comment? (Fr.) what do you mean?

It was like Europe in the Middle Ages Again the considered analogy with the past, implying a primitive and crude society.

innocence is like a dumb leper who has lost his bell Note the effectiveness of the image – the bell warned others not to approach. Greene was to write about a leper colony in a later novel, *A Burnt-Out Case* (1961).

Deux Américains? (Fr.) two Americans (are they here)?

the Sunday of the body Superb phrase to indicate that the girls have a rest day because the troops who would normally buy their favours are confined to barracks.

poach on military territory i.e. this place was frequented by soldiers.

Je suis un vieux ... vigoureux (Fr.) I am an old man ... too tired. My friend ... he is very rich, very virile.

Tu es sale (Fr.) you are a dirty old man.

piastres and greenbacks i.e. currency in use locally *and* American dollar bills.

je suis un Anglais ... pauvre (Fr.) I am English, poor, very poor.

popular in Paris five years ago A pathetic indication of how far behind the times everything is in this area.

Banque de l'Indo-Chine The Indo-Chinese Bank.

the eighteenth-century future i.e. they properly belonged to the age of rationalism, as the description of them suggests.

Augustans i.e. verses, usually in couplets.

Wordsworth William Wordsworth (1770–1850) the great poet of the English Romantic movement, forever associated with the Lake District (see the reference in the next sentence to 'English lakes').

C'est impardonable (Fr.) it's unforgiveable.

Peut-on avoir l'honneur? (Fr.) may I have the honour (pleasure) (of this dance)?

and a settlement i.e. a sum of money.

electrical sewing machines for starving seamstresses Note the irony again – Fowler has sometimes an acid tongue – but he is really getting at the ineffectuality of the aid, and perhaps even at its irrelevance.

like a chairman with his gavel Miss Hei is indicating that that there is a certain order of proceedings, and she intends to have them observed.

steak tartare i.e. rare steak with a savoury sauce containing mayonnaise, chopped gherkins etc.

a mandarin in Hué See earlier note and the section on 'Background'.

Singapore The island at the extreme tip of the Malay peninsula, a centre for commerce and trading, one of the jewels of the East.

communal closet i.e. shared toilet.

A newspaper scoop? i.e. a story printed before other papers get it.

Korea Peninsula extending from the East Asian mainland towards Japan.

War broke out between North and South Korea in 1950 with the Chinese assisting the North Koreans and the United Nations the South Koreans. A truce was reached between the two sides in 1953.

Sometimes she seemed invisible like peace. Another example of Greene's superbly economic statements, though here with a touch of cynicism.

Chapter 4

Section 1

The reader is again taken back in time as Fowler describes an earlier visit to Phat Diem; at that time the town was still held by the French though it was surrounded by the enemy. This account explains much that becomes apparent in Fowler's character later, namely his wish not to be committed but merely to report. This stems from the horrors he experienced here, horrors which would unhinge the committed man's sanity. He recalls his own memories of Phat Diem, with its tremendous Catholic influence: he notes that although the enemy had been pushed back half a mile, the whole town seemed to be in or near the precincts of the massive cathedral, as if this were their only protection. Fowler remembers talking to the priest, who also acted as overworked surgeon to the wounded.

Later Fowler left to go out with a French patrol; this is perhaps the most cathartic experience of his life. In a canal they found hundreds of floating bodies 'I am reminded now of an Irish stew containing too much meat.' They managed to cross the canal despite the 'shoal of bodies', and when they later neared a farmhouse they found a woman and child dead. Fowler thought 'I hate war.' He spent the night with the French officers, and discussed their chances of holding on to what they had got with them. Fowler then fell asleep, dreamed of Pyle, and awoke to find that Pyle had arrived to join him.

Section 2

Pyle revealed the purpose behind his journey (for which he had even purchased a boat): he was in love with Phuong and wished to marry her. He was relieved by the calm manner in which Fowler accepted the news, and they continued to talk throughout the mortar attacks. Again Greene makes us aware of the interrelation-ship in time as Fowler, returning to the present, observes that after Pyle's death 'Time has its revenges.' They had finished that earlier night together drinking whisky but 'saying nothing'.

Textual notes, Sections 1–2

like a panorama ... *Illustrated London News* A famous largely picture magazine which covered world-wide events, particularly events in the British Empire, hence the reference to the Boer War in South Africa (1899–1902).

calcaire Limestone.

breviary i.e. the book containing the Divine Office for each day.

Senegalese i.e. from the French Colony of Senegal in West Africa.

London thoroughfare ... all-clear ... 'Unexploded Bomb' This time the nostalgia is for the London of wartime, with the 'all-clear' siren sounding after an air-raid.

Freemason Member of the fraternity of Masons for mutual help and brotherly feeling having elaborate secret rituals and signs.

amity Friendship.

monstrance The open or transparent vessel of gold or silver in which the Host is exposed.

more Buddhist than Christian Note the curious combination in the description of the unlikely coming together of East and West. Buddhism originated in India in the fifth century BC.

Low Country i.e. like Belgium and the Netherlands.

Tonkin plain See section on 'Background'.

Etat Major (Fr.) General Staff.

a great King i.e. God.

soutane Priest's cassock.

I wanted to get my bearings i.e. find out where I am.

A light flashed i.e. a signal lamp, probably using Morse code.

sten guns Light, portable machine guns much used in the Second World War.

the long antennae of a walkie-talkie An imaginative description of the use of short-range radio communication between troops.

deploy i.e. arrange ourselves.

I am reminded now of an Irish stew containing too much meat Note how the homely image contrasts with the grotesqueness of the actual slaughter.

seal-grey ... a convict with a shaven scalp The image – the killing of seals and imprisonment – is a dual indictment of the *crime* of war.

Gott sei dank (Ger.) thank God.

oleographs Pictures printed in oils.

cadavers Corpses.

over-prepared the event i.e. expected something to happen (for which he had prepared himself) but which did not in the event take place.

Deux civils (Fr.) two civilians.

Mal chance (Fr.) bad luck.

the juju i.e. the superstition, here equated cynically with religious faith by Fowler.

a bazooka An anti-tank rocket-gun; the name was coined from a comical musical instrument.

Captain Sorel The choice of name is ironic, since Julian Sorel, the hero of Stendhal's *Le Rouge et le Noir* has to choose between the military and religious life.

any concentrations i.e. large gatherings of troops.

(I was reminded of ... the arras) Hamlet stabs Polonius, who is listening behind the arras, in Act III, scene 4.

barnstormers i.e. strolling players, ranting actors, an echo of *Hamlet* again, for the players enact the drama before the court in Act III, scene 2.

"A" certificate The now outdated censorship classification of films, meaning that it was suitable for adults, and children only if accompanied by an adult.

He had in his hand ... respectability A clear indication of the nature of Phuong's ambition – perhaps more correctly her sister's – and at the same time a considered stress on Pyle's far wider deception which is hidden behind this respectability.

swell, swell i.e. good, first-rate, understanding.

Lowell or a Cabot Two of the most celebratedly snobbish of Boston families. They were the subject of a witty rhyme.

straight i.e. a person of integrity, honest.

the Anglo-Saxon word Of four letters indicating sexual intercourse. Still considered low in usage, though perhaps made almost respectable since the acceptance of an uncensored version of D. H. Lawrence's *Lady Chatterley's Lover*.

a favourable rate of exchange i.e. good value for your money.

Time has its revenges 'And thus the whirligig of time brings in his revenges' (*Twelfth Night*, V,1,388).

bamboozle i.e. deceive.

leader-writers i.e. those who write the leader columns in the papers.

Chapter 5

Section 1

Fowler recalls that at the time he had only intended being absent
from Saigon for a week. However, because the road had been cut,
he was unable to return to Saigon for three weeks. Pyle, of course,
had managed to get through and return to Saigon immediately.
Fowler found a letter from Pyle awaiting him at Hanoi: in it, he
again praised Fowler for the calmness with which he had received
the news and vowed that he would not see Phuong until Fowler
was also back in Saigon. Whilst in Hanoi, Fowler had attended a
press conference given by a French colonel. It appeared the French
had the enemy on the run though the colonel was unwillingly to
reveal to Granger, who was also present, the casualties his troops
had suffered. Granger's baiting eventually led the colonel to
recriminate the Americans for not dropping the supplies they had
promised.

On arriving back in Saigon, Fowler learns by telegram that he
has been appointed the paper's new Foreign Editor. However the
new post entailed a return to England, thus leaving Phuong to Pyle.

I must get a shine i.e. have my shoes cleaned and polished.

sterling qualities ... dollar love Cynical word-play on currency
values.

Junior A reference to the American proclivity of calling sons in a family
'Junior' (e.g. John Junior).

Mother's Day Fourth Sunday in Lent.

Reno In the state of Nevada, it is renowned for the speed with which
divorces can be arranged.

the Virgin Islands A group of islands in the West Indies.

pointer Stick, indicator.

web of evasion A phrase which draws parallels with Pyle's misguided
evasions.

Left-Wing deputies i.e. Communist.

Ho Chi Minh Communist leader. See section on 'Background'.

St Cyr French military academy for officers established in 1808 in the
former school for girls set up by Louis XIV and Madame de Maintenon.

cartes de Noël i.e. Christmas cards.

gangrene i.e. decomposition of part of the body usually caused by an
obstruction in the circulation.

Interpretez (Fr.) you translate.

Got him on the raw i.e. where it hurt, caught him unexpectedly.

Dante never thought ... promoted to Purgatory A reference to *The Divine Comedy* of Dante (1265–1321), of which the Purgatorio is a part. The lovers of the poem were Paolo and Francesca, and Fowler is ironically comparing himself and Phuong to this pair.

Lord Salisbury Robert, 3rd Marquis of Salisbury (1830–1903) British statesman, three times Prime Minister in the nineteenth century.

card ... trumps Note the use of a small but effective imagery sequence.

Pax Bar i.e. Peace Bar.

Corsican From the island of Corsica in the Mediterranean, under French jurisdiction.

Marseilles The large French Mediterranean port.

Home ... England Note again the ironic, somewhat cynical attitude of Fowler.

Part two

Chapter 1

Section 1

Back in Saigon, Pyle pays a visit to Fowler. Phuong, however does not want to be present at the meeting and decides to visit her sister. While awaiting Pyle's arrival, Fowler writes to his editor requesting that he be allowed to remain in Vietnam as their correspondent. When he arrives, Fowler questions Pyle about the plastic that he has been importing into the country: Pyle maintains that it is being brought in to aid local industry.

Fowler finds Pyle's determined respectability and narrowness difficult to handle and is irritated by Pyle's dog. Phuong returns and Pyle declares his love for her – Fowler has to act as translator as Pyle cannot speak French. There follows a somewhat bitter exchange and Pyle, angered by Fowler's baiting, asks Phuong to go away with him. However, Phuong does not wish to go with Pyle and he leaves. Fowler now writes to his wife asking her for a divorce.

like the missing letters on a Roman tomb i.e. worn away by time.

Reuter's The international news agency founded by Baron Reuter which
conveyed news by telegraph.

General de Lattre See section on 'Background'.

Hong Kong dateline See earlier note on Paris dateline p.35.

Streatham South-west suburb of London.

a Hawaii shirt i.e. probably floral and in loud colours.

On the rocks On ice cubes.

the Black Prince The Prince of Wales (1330–76), son of Edward III,
distinguished himself at the battles of Crécy and Poitiers. He is said to
have won his popular title from the black armour he wore.

Limoges 375 km (250 miles) south of Paris, mercilessly sacked in 1370
by the Black Prince, who was by then worn out by sickness.

Duke's toilet i.e. his cleaning of his private parts.

Connecticut One of the New England States in the USA.

run amok i.e. go berserk, run mad.

dumb i.e. simple, ignorant.

kidding i.e. joking.

Enchantée (Fr.) delighted i.e. delighted to make your acquaintance.

and dice for her Since Fowler gambles, this is an appropriate image.
It also reduces Phuong to an impersonal object – as indeed she is.

horoscope i.e. what the stars foretell – Fowler is continuing a little acidly
in his sarcastic vein.

Avec moi (Fr.) with me.

Occidental Of or belonging to the West, or Europe, as opposed to
oriental.

skyscrapers i.e. multiple storey buildings, they dominate the skyline of
New York.

tube-trains i.e. underground.

the Statue of Liberty This statue commands the entrance to New York
harbour.

Chapter 2

Section 1

The chapter opens with a description of the Caodaist festival at
Tanyin, which by chance both Fowler and Pyle attend. Fowler
spots Pyle talking to a commandant in General Thé's army: it
appears his car has broken down and the commandant can arrange
for a mechanic. To escape the heat, Fowler enters the cathedral.

On coming out, he finds that Pyle is still with the commandant and nothing has been done about his car. Fowler offers him a lift.

Section 2

Fowler now discovers that the petrol has been siphoned out of his car and six miles out of Tanyin, it breaks down. They are within thirty yards of a watch tower and decide to seek shelter for the night.

Section 3

In the tower they find two frightened Vietnamese supposedly on guard duty but terrified at the thought of a Communist patrol launching an attack on their particular watch tower (there are forty such towers between them and Saigon). Fowler and Pyle talk of religion and Pyle reveals that he is an Unitarian. In an attempt to befriend the guards, Pyle gives them cigarettes. Pyle's talk with Fowler reveals his obsessions about the state of affairs in the East, in particular his dislike of colonialism. He is unable to accept Fowler's lack of commitment, because he himself is so committed.

Fowler leaves the tower to collect a blanket from his car; using Fowler's return to the tower as a diversion, Pyle succeeds in getting the sten gun away from the guards. Pyle now feels a good deal safer and resumes his conversation with Fowler: they discuss Phuong and Fowler is moved to confide his fears of impending old age and death. Suddenly they hear a voice through a loudspeaker urging the guards to give up the civilians. Fowler and Pyle decide to make a run for it. As they start out for the field, they hear a bazooka shell burst on the tower.

Section 4

As a result of the explosion Fowler is injured in the leg, and is dependent on Pyle to help him get away from the scene; they escape through the paddy fields, with Pyle half-carrying the crippled Fowler. They watch Fowler's car burn after being hit by the firing. Pyle is moved to confess that he could not leave Fowler to die because of Phuong – 'When you are in love you want to play the game, that's all.' Pyle goes for help, and returns; Fowler, is given an injection of morphia to ease the pain in his leg.

Textual notes, Sections 1–4

Holy See The episcopal unit committed to the Bishop or Archbishop.
Confucian Pertaining to Confucius the Chinese philosopher (551–479 BC).
planchette Small board supported by two castors and a pencil which, when a person's fingers rest lightly on the board, is said to trace letters without conscious direction.
Saint Victor Hugo See section on 'Background'. Hugo (1802–85) was the great French novelist, poet and playwright whose works included *Les Misérables*, a panoramic piece of social history.
Walt Disney (1901–66) the celebrated cartoonist and producer of cartoon films, universally known as the creator of Mickey Mouse.
a two-star general Fairly low in the hierarchy, and consequently often an administrator rather than a field general.
C.D. Corps Diplomatique.
Moroccans i.e. French troops from French Morocco in North Africa.
curfew i.e. the time that everyone has to be in by.
like a green bowler hat Note the incongruity and again the nostalgia of the image.
chinoiserie An imitation of Chinese motifs.
Los Angeles American city in Southern California.
the Great Pyramid Of Cheops at Giza west of Cairo.
phoney i.e. false.
Buick American make of motor car, generally of a large variety.
air of Tanyin ... too ethical Fowler is being sarcastic because of Pyle's pomposity.
thermos i.e. a flask for keeping liquid either hot or cold.
Vit-Health Typical advertising, Vit being short for the vitamins supposedly contained in the product.
Rome – or Canterbury The two great centres, the first of the Catholic religion, the second of the Protestant religion.
French Academy Of forty members, founded by Richelieu in 1635, it is charged with the interests of French language and literature.
Sun Yat Sen (1866–1925) the great Chinese revolutionary who after several unsuccessful uprisings was victorious in the revolution of 1911. Acknowledged as the father of the Chinese republic by all political factions.

Gurkha patrol i.e. of Gurkha soldiers from Nepal, stalwarts in the British Army.

Pahang As in the text, a mining area in Malaya.

like weights on a balance Appropriate image, and later the scales tip against Fowler and Pyle.

Honor The Americanized spelling.

Gas Gasolene, petrol.

C'est défendu (Fr.) it is forbidden.

but a postcard of sky Again the nostalgic image – postcards come from home.

one of those mugs i.e. simpletons.

Extrême Orient i.e. the *Far East*, the name of a newspaper.

Unitarian Member of a religious body which does not hold with the doctrine of the Trinity that there are three persons in one god.

Bangkok Capital of Siam (Thailand).

Berkeleian From George Berkeley (1685–1753) Anglican Bishop and philosopher.

a megaphone i.e. a device which makes the voice louder.

Indo-China goes ... Siam goes i.e. falls to the Communists, supported by the Chinese.

enlisted i.e. conscripted, and more particularly without a commission.

like a monk's flagellation i.e. self-chastisement to teach humility in the sight of God.

lowered i.e. scowled.

Burma British colony, granted independence in 1947.

engagé (Fr.) committed.

La liberté ... la liberté? (Fr.) freedom – what does freedom consist of?

global strategy i.e. manoeuvres of the great powers, here Russia and America.

I don't like Ike A reversal of the slogan – I like Ike – which was used in support of Dwight D. Eisenhower (1890–1969) and his campaign for the Presidency. Standing as a Republican, he was elected President in 1952 and was re-elected in 1956.

Je reviens ... suite (Fr.) I'll be back as quickly as possible.

Gordon Square See the earlier note on Bloomsbury – it is in the same vicinity, and again Fowler is indulging his nostalgia.

Venus ... Bears ... Southern Cross All the names of stars and used to great effect here to point to the smallness of man and his wars against the vastness of space.

Somebody's had it i.e. been killed.

Touché i.e. a point to you.

Paris-Match French picture magazine.

No barricado for a belly See *A Winter's Tale*, I,2,204.

to go into whistling See note p.39 on 'wolf-whistles'.

the Kinsey Report A. C. Kinsey (1898–1956) published a series of case histories under the title *Sexual Behaviour in the Human Male* (1948).

the blitz i.e. the air-attacks on London in particular during the Second World War (1939–45).

Chink i.e. a Chinese.

what mental age Private soldiers in the American army were classified according to their mental ability.

cliché A stale or over-used phrase, a platitude.

ran off the customary rails? i.e. were unpredictable.

G.I.s American soldiers (after 1943), the term was coined from 'general issue' kit.

ultimatum i.e. order with a fixed time in which it must be obeyed.

crooners i.e. popular singers. Bing Crosby was the great example.

like a picture on the screen A vivid and appropriate image, for much of war and incidents of war like this are 'screened'.

a knacker's yard i.e. where horses are slaughtered.

the painless killer i.e. a gun held at the head.

we were like awkward … race Even at this moment of crisis there is a sense of the grotesque.

like a banker's bid Pyle has, in fact, offered Phuong the security of marriage and respectability.

the elaborate cypher of the constellations i.e. the code of the stars which have their own time and purpose in space 'which I couldn't read' – that is, not understood by man.

Je suis Frongçais In Pyle's atrocious accent, 'I am French.'

hypodermic of morphia i.e. injection of morphine which alleviates pain.

Chapter 3

Section 1

Fowler returns to Phuong, his leg in splints. He learns that her sister Miss Hei is now working for the Americans. In his absence, a letter has arrived from his wife Helen: she refuses to divorce him. Fowler now writes to Pyle thanking him for saving his life and telling him that his wife 'has more or less agreed to divorce me' – a blatant lie.

Section 2

This contains a brief account of Fowler's assistant Dominguez, his
illness at this time, and the value of his contacts: Fowler now has to
personally attend the wearisome Press Conferences in his place and
listen to local gossip in the bars. However, the sick Dominguez is
still able to come up with some useful leads on Pyle's activities.
Fowler follows these up and visits a certain Mr Chou in his warehouse. However, once there he discovers that Mr Heng the warehouse manager, is the source of information. He shows Fowler some
moulds which Pyle is supplying to General Thé along with an
American plastic called Diolacton. Although he will not explain the
significance of these materials, Heng is keen that Fowler should
know that the Americans are supplying it to General Thé. Heng's
sympathies clearly lie with the Vietminh and he goes on to explain
that 'If anything unpleasant happens here in Saigon, it will be
blamed on us. My Committee would like you to take a fair view.'

Section 3

Pyle pays an unwelcome visit to Fowler. Pyle has learned from
Miss Hei of Fowler's promotion and of his wife's refusal to divorce
him: he is angry that Fowler should have lied to him. Fowler
questions his scruples and brings up the subject of plastics though
unfortunately Pyle provides no further leads. Finally he tells Pyle to
leave 'Go to your Third Force and York Harding and the Rôle
of Democracy. Go away and play with plastics.'

Textual notes, Sections 1–3

urinoir (Fr.) lavatory.
carrying Fate in the lines ... on the palm Their destiny – and what
  they had suffered – was as plain on their faces as the fortunes of others
  are clear to the reader of palms.
like a coolie i.e. a labourer in the East.
Corinne ... François ... Mme Bompierre As we should expect, a
  French film.
She had found the dried scab i.e. she has found his weakest and most
  vulnerable spot, the fact that he had left Anne in time.
dégagé i.e. uncommitted.

like a dog on a crusader's tomb A vivid image, and Phuong is not much more animated.

like an ant meeting an obstacle Fowler is only temporarily baulked, and now tells the lie about his wife's being ready to divorce him.

Goa A Portuguese possession 400 km (250 miles) south-east of Bombay.

Krishna Hindu divinity.

Batu Caves A place of pilgrimage on the border of Kuala Lumpur and Malaya.

Boulevard A large street or thoroughfare.

Congressmen i.e. from the United States Assembly.

Hawaii, Puerto Rico … New Mexico The first a group of volcanic islands in the North Pacific, the second an island in the West Indies, the third a state of the USA.

Quai (Fr.) quay.

Boulevard de la Somme A street named after the famous battle of the First World War.

a pantomime set i.e. the stage and its backcloth ready for the Christmas pantomime – probably, in view of the Chinese setting, Greene is thinking of *Aladdin*.

sampans Small boats with stern-oars used for carrying supplies – or arms.

godown Warehouse

Picasso Pablo Picasso (1881–1973) was the Spanish born painter who dominated much of early 20th-century French art. He was the founder of Cubism.

jackdaw's nest of a house Jackdaws collect any and everything with which to make their nests. The implication is that the house is in a mess.

mah jongg A Chinese game for four players with 144 pieces called tiles, much played in Europe and America from the mid 1920s onwards.

Café de la Paix Café of Peace. The name implies some wishful thinking on the part of the proprietor.

the tiny crippled feet of old China A reference to the time when Chinese girls had their feet bound from childhood onwards in order to keep them small and dainty.

within the smoky corridors of his skull A fine way of suggesting that he is 'hooked' on opium.

the ordeal by tea As distinct from the Chinese torture of 'ordeal by water'.

expectoration Spit.

palaeolithic A reference to the period when primitive stone implements were used.

saviour i.e. who had saved me – but the term has ironic Christian associations.

possum Still; from the opossum's habit of feigning death if attacked.

Silence like a plant put out tendrils Another fine image which conveys the spread of silence.

Le cauchemar? (Fr.) the nightmare?

the formula of intercourse The pattern of love-making.

state coach ... Westminster The coach is used for state occasions, for example the opening of Parliament – hence its name.

a comfortable lay i.e. Phuong is a convenience at hand to be made love to.

desire ... weapon ... womb Notice the sexual nature of the imagery, which conveys Fowler's 'savage' lovemaking to Phuong.

Je ne comprends pas (Fr.) I don't understand.

Part three

Chapter 1

Section 1

We now move forward in time: it is a fortnight since Pyle's death. Fowler meets Vigot who is still pursuing his investigations. They quote Pascal at each other and Vigot asks if he might be allowed to call on Fowler that evening.

Section 2

We now move back in time to the period immediately after Pyle's departure (Chapter 3,3): Fowler is jealous of Pyle and begins running down all things American. There now follows the bicycle bombs fiasco: following up a lead given to him by Heng, Fowler visits a garage in search of the moulds he had seen earlier at Chou's warehouse. Fowler realizes that the Americans are supplying bombs to General Thé and that these are being moved around Saigon in bicycle pumps. All the newspapers which cover the bicycle bombs incident blame the Vietminh; only Fowler lays the responsibility on General Thé and even his copy is changed by the office to read Vietminh. He apologizes to Heng. After his unsuccessful search of the garage, Fowler returns home to find that Phuong has packed up her possessions and left.

Section 3

Fowler pays a visit to the American Legation in search of Pyle. Unfortunately Pyle is not there but Fowler does gain some satisfaction in launching a verbal attack on Miss Hei who works as a typist for the Economic Attaché.

Section 4

Fowler now travels north and accompanies a French pilot on a bombing raid near the Chinese border. After the relentless bombing, the pilot shoots up a solitary sampan much to Fowler's disgust.

Section 5

Trouin, the pilot, then takes Fowler on to an opium den. They discuss the war and the sampan and later Trouin sets Fowler up with an expensive prostitute. Unfortunately, the memory of Phuong is too strong and at the moment of sexual communion, Fowler is impotent.

Textual notes, Sections 1–5

partisan i.e. an active member of a resistance group.

protected like caterpillars This refers to their camouflaged uniforms.

Sans vaseline (Fr.) without lubrication (part of the sexual jargon referred to in the next line). It probably means 'easily'.

Sous-lieutenant Equivalent to Second-Lieutenant.

Gaboriau Emile Gaboriau (1832–73), the father of French detective fiction and the creator of the character 'Lecoq'.

Loneliness lay in my bed Note the effectiveness of the personification, which brings home to Fowler the sense of his loss.

napalm i.e. a bomb containing jellied petrol.

zareba A hedged or palisaded enclosure for protection.

Operation Bicyclette A parody of the high-flown titles given to attacks and counter-attacks in war.

A bicycle wheel hummed like a top Another facet of Greene's style, the essentially cinematic or visual quality.

Eiffel Tower The famous Paris landmark.

still a press i.e. a terrible crowd.

twitter of the hedges Note the use of nature in Greene's imagery which conveys an insubstantial quality – for life is cheap.

à propos i.e. relevant, appropriate.

innuendoes Suggestions.

rake-off i.e. payment, cut, commission.

American Consul ... Scientist The American representative and the approval of the Christian Science movement.

Squadron Gascogne Air Force unit, perhaps from Gascony.

aperitif An alcoholic drink taken before a meal which acts as an appetizer.

Southend Pier Presumably because it is the longest in this country, though now it faces possible closure.

B.26 bombers i.e. made by Boeing in the United States, the B standing for the manufacturers.

Great Racer at the Wembley Exhibition One of the many attractions of the fun-fair at the British Empire Exhibition (1924–5).

detour A roundabout trip, away from the main area.

Baie d'Along On the coast of northern Indo-China.

helmeted Martian The helmet conceals the human face and thus appears impersonal.

métisse Of mixed race, in this case probably white and Chinese.

The men of Vichy When the Germans occupied France in 1940, they set up a puppet French government in Vichy, of which Pétain and Laval were the chief members.

at the moment of entry i.e. sexual penetration by the male.

Chapter 2

Section 1

Fowler returns to Saigon and goes to his flat. Pyle opens the door to him: he had met Dominguez delivering the mail and had asked to be allowed to await Fowler's return. Fowler reads a letter from his editor saying that he can stay in Indo-China for at least another year. Fowler asks Pyle, as Pyle might have said a month before, to go easy on Phuong. He then admits, much to his own surprise, that he is glad that Phuong has chosen Pyle to settle down with.

Fowler now goes in search of a new flat as the old one holds too many memories. He meets a collector of erotic art who tries to sell him a flat with the collection thrown in. Afterwards Fowler goes to the Pavilion for a drink. Suddenly there is a terrible explosion in the square outside the bar. In the chaos which follows the explosion, Fowler views with horror the dead, the dying and the mutilated.

Pyle is also there and the awful realization that the bomb is Pyle's responsibility suddenly dawns on Fowler. Unbeknown to Pyle, the military parade which should have taken place had been cancelled the day before (Pyle had not known as he had been out of town the day before) and the bomb's victims are innocent women and children – the bomb had gone off at Saigon's peak shopping period. Fowler curses Pyle and his Third Force, and considers him the dupe of General Thé. As the terrible sights of the victims come back to him, Fowler realizes how deeply he hates the war and its consequences and that no matter how hard he fights it, he is indeed committed.

Textual notes, Sections 1–2

We shall keep the chair warm for you i.e. the job will be waiting when you return.

Canasta Card game of South American origin resembling rummy.

Perhaps there is a prophet i.e. perhaps we sense what is going to happen (in this case, perhaps, Fowler senses Pyle's impending death).

crachin (Fr.) fine rain which soaks one to the skin.

Rops Felicien Rops (1833–98) was a Belgian artist known for his lithographs and etchings. He achieved some reknown for his illustrations to the works of Baudelaire and it is probably these that the planter has hanging in the bathroom.

Aphrodite Probably an erotic book.

Nana A novel by Emile Zola (1840–1902).

La Garçonne See note on *Aphrodite* above.

Paul de Kock (1794–1871) a French novelist who wrote numerous novels which were somewhat 'piquant' in their day.

like a tourist glutted with churches i.e. who has seen too many.

deodorants ... sterilized Again Fowler's obsession with the American obsession with personal hygiene.

porto Port.

cointreau ... chartreuse ... pastis Various reinforced alcoholic drinks.

Part four
Chapter 1

The reader again moves forward in time: Fowler, in anticipation of Vigot's proposed visit, sends Phuong to the cinema with her sister. Fowler finds himself relating to Vigot as if he (Vigot) were a priest hearing confession. They go through the events of the night that Pyle died and Vigot indicates the little inaccuracies in Fowler's story. The inspector suspects that Fowler saw Pyle on that evening as the traces of cement found between Pyle's dog's paws suggest a visit to Fowler's flat. However Fowler, despite his own inward admissions, will not reveal what happened.

Chapter 2

Section 1

In this section Fowler relates the actual events of that evening. He visits Heng to confirm that Pyle was indeed responsible for the explosion in the square and indicates the need to stop Pyle from any further action. Heng agrees to 'talk' to Pyle for it is apparent that Fowler is obsessed by the killings.

Section 2

Fowler leaves a note for Pyle inviting him round for drinks. Whilst awaiting the latter's arrival, Dominguez arrives at the door: he has come to file a follow up story on the explosion, but Fowler tells him that he is still too shocked by the incident to think in terms of sending cables and asks Dominguez to do it for him. Pyle arrives shortly after Dominguez's departure: he has reprimanded Thé and told him that should such an incident occur again, the Americans will be obliged to withdraw their support. Fowler is horrified that they should still contemplate supporting Thé. He now determines to follow up Heng's suggestion and invites Pyle to dine at the Vieux Moulin: he then signals to Heng's man outside that Pyle has accepted the invitation. Fowler offers Pyle a drink and the 'quiet American' is soon in a talking mood. Pyle justifies his actions to Fowler and even refers to the dead in the square as 'war casualties'.

Section 3

Following Pyle's departure, Fowler goes to the Majestic where he sees Wilkins, then to a cinema, which he leaves for the Vieux Moulin. There he meets Granger who appears to be glaring at him malevolently. It turns out that Granger is in search of some sympathy for he has just learned that his son has got polio. Fowler goes down into the street where he finds Phuong waiting in a doorway. We are back at the beginning of the story.

Textual notes, Sections 1–3

Il faut ... Heng It is imperative that I see Monsieur Heng.

O.S.S. Office of Strategic Services.

Harvard The oldest and first university of the United States. It was founded in 1638.

those who had learnt ... into candles Nero was Roman Emperor from AD 54 to 68, infamous for his excesses and the burning and persecution of Christians.

Darwin manuscripts Presumably either Charles (1809–82) famous author of *The Origin of Species* or any of his talented scientific sons, one of whom worked in the same area as Professor Pyle – i.e. tides, rotating masses etc.

isolationist Politically, not committed to supporting any particular movement and not interfering in the internal affairs of another nation.

alibi An account of one's behaviour elsewhere during the time an alleged act happened.

Russell ... Times A reference to Sir William Russell (1821–1907) who was war correspondent of *The Times* at the time of the Crimean War

(1854–5) and later sent despatches on the Indian Mutiny and the American Civil War.

The lamps shone o'er fair women and brave men The quotation is from Lord Byron's *Childe Harold's Pilgrimage* Canto 3, an account of The Duchess of Richmond's ball the night before the battle of Waterloo in June 1815.

Errol Flynn … Tyrone Power Two romantic actors successful in a number of Hollywood films from the mid 1930s onwards.

Oedipus … Thebes A reference to the central figure in Greek tragedy, who was fated to kill his father and marry his mother; the latter Jocasta hanged herself, Oedipus went mad and put out his own eyes.

Burgundian i.e. from Burgundy.

Chapon duc Charles A recipe for cooking a capon.

one body can contain all the suffering the world can feel A fine focus of microcosmic intensity.

pissed Drunk.

Limies i.e. Britishers.

stomachs i.e. puts up with.

Pittsburgh A port in S.W. Pennyslvania, known as the steel city.

poufs i.e. homosexuals.

polio i.e. poliomyelitis, which at the time was more widespread than it is now, and often left the sufferer handicapped or crippled.

mopping-up i.e. clearing out the last troops of the enemy.

Chapter 3

Phuong asks Fowler if Vigot has been to see him, and then tells Fowler about the film she has seen, which was about the French Revolution. Fowler pretends that things are just as they were, and then reads a telegram from Helen saying that she has thought things over and is prepared to divorce him. Phuong is excited, and obviously has no thoughts for the dead Pyle; but Fowler himself is filled with remorse: although all is well now in his world, Fowler has no one in whom he can confide or express his regret to.

French Revolution This began with the storming of the Bastille on 14 July 1789.

Marseillaise The hymn or march of the French Republicans was composed, words and music, by Roget de Lisle one night in April 1792. It later became the French National Anthem.

Une aristocrate A female aristocrat (i.e. for the guillotine).

The Empire State Building ... the Cheddar Gorge ... the Grand Canyon The first is one of the sights of New York, the second a modestly spectacular geographical feature in Somerset, the third a truly spectacular gorge of the Colorado river in North Arizona, USA over 320 km (200 miles) long and 1·6 km (1 mile) deep.

General questions

1 Write a detailed character sketch of Alden Pyle, saying whether or not you consider him to be a sympathetic character.

2 Referring widely to examples from the text, indicate the nature of the *figurative* language used in this novel.

3 By referring to specific incidents, give an account of Fowler's reactions to the war in Indo-China.

4 Indicate the part played by Phuong in this novel. In what ways do you consider her to be a positive character?

5 By close analysis of certain scenes, show how Graham Greene creates atmosphere in *The Quiet American*.

6 By looking closely at certain situations and reactions, indicate whether you think that Fowler is merely a reporter in *The Quiet American*.

7 What are the advantages – and disadvantages – of using the first person narrative only in a novel of this kind? You should quote from the text in support of your views.

8 In what ways is Greene's technique in this novel similar to that of techniques used in film-making? You should refer to specific instances in your answer.

9 Compare and contrast the characters of Vigot and Granger.

10 Write an essay on what is meant by *innocence* in *The Quiet American*.

11 By detailed reference to two or three chapters, show how Greene integrates the past into the present in this novel.

12 In what ways is Graham Greene a realistic writer? You should quote in support of your views.

13 In what ways do you find Fowler a sympathetic character? You should refer closely to the novel in support of your views.

14 Write an essay on either (a) the use of French or (b) the importance of the literary references in *The Quiet American*.

15 Although Greene stresses that this is a story, indicate the importance of the political and historical background to a full appreciation of this novel.